MIND BOGGLES

PUZZLES, RIDDLES, AND TRICKS TO BLOW YOUR MIND!

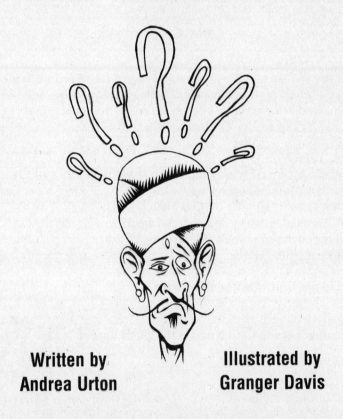

Written by
Andrea Urton

Illustrated by
Granger Davis

Lowell House
Juvenile
Los Angeles

CONTEMPORARY BOOKS

Chicago

*To Ruby Dutcher, for her patience
during the creation of this book*
—A.U.

For Roger and Jessica
—G.D.

PUBLISHER: Jack Artenstein
GENERAL MANAGER, JUVENILE DIVISION: Elizabeth Duell Wood
EDITORIAL DIRECTOR: Brenda Pope-Ostrow
PROJECT EDITORS: Carolyn Wendt and Lisa Melton
DIRECTOR OF PUBLISHING SERVICES: Mary D. Aarons
TEXT DESIGN: Lisa-Theresa Lenthall and Carolyn Wendt
COVER PHOTOGRAPH: Tom Nelson

Manufactured in the United States of America

ISBN: 1-56565-176-6
Library of Congress Catalog Card Number: 94-28861

10 9 8 7 6 5 4 3 2

Lowell House books can be purchased at special discounts when ordered in bulk for premiums and special sales. Contact Department VH at the following address:

Lowell House Juvenile
2029 Century Park East
Suite 3290
Los Angeles, CA 90067

CONTENTS

PUZZLING PARADOXES

WHAT IS A PARADOX?

No, it's not two surgeons getting together for lunch. A paradox is an idea, statement, or situation that seems to contradict itself or seems to be completely illogical or contrary to common sense. For example, a sign that says "DON'T READ THIS" is paradoxical because you must read it first to find out that you are not supposed to read it!

The strange thing about paradoxes is that they just can't be resolved. Once you think you have one figured out, you find yourself saying, "But if that's true, then what about . . . ?" And around and around you go!

Read on and see if you and your friends can solve these mind-boggling paradoxes.

CROSS MY HEART AND HOPE TO LIE

Suppose you've just met a Martian who claims that "all Martians are liars." If what he says is true, then, because he is a Martian, he must be lying, so nothing he says is true. Therefore, the statement "all Martians are liars" must be a lie. But how can it be a lie if it is true? And that takes you right back to where you started!

SPLITTING HAIRS

In Smithville, U.S.A., there is only one barber. He shaves all of the men in town who do not shave themselves. In fact, he shaves *only* the men in town who do not shave themselves. Given that, ask yourself: Who shaves the barber?

It can't be that he shaves himself, since he shaves only men who do *not* shave themselves. But if he shaves *all* the men in town who do not shave themselves, a group that would include the barber himself, he *must* shave himself. Could the answer be that the barber has a beard? No, that would still put him in with the group of men who do not shave themselves— and he shaves all of them. Think about it!

Probably one of the most famous paradoxes is in the question, "Which came first, the chicken or the egg?" What's the answer?

THE INCREDIBLE SHRINKING FROG

There are even paradoxes in nature. The development of the paradoxical frog is truly puzzling. This creature begins life as one of the largest known tadpoles—about 7 inches long. No one knows why, but during its transformation into an adult, the frog actually shrinks! The adult is a mere 2.2 inches long.

HI, GRANDPA!

There are many scientists who believe some sort of time travel will one day be possible. But traveling back in time could cause some very sticky problems! One snag that must be faced has come to be known as the Grandfather Paradox.

What would happen if you traveled into the past, met your grandfather before he had had any children, and then, by some freak accident, you caused his death? Obviously, if your (now dead) grandfather had never had children, then you could never have been born. But if you had never been born, you could not have traveled back in time and accidentally killed your grandfather. How do you explain *that*?!

THE SWAMI'S DILEMMA

If you are asked to answer yes or no to a question, you have a 50 percent chance of being correct. Right? Well, not always, as is shown in a paradox called the Swami's Prediction. A woman bets a famous swami that he cannot predict the future. The woman writes something on a piece of paper, folds it in half, then asks the swami to decide whether the event described on the paper will occur by five o'clock. She tells the swami to write yes or no on the same piece of paper. The swami chooses no.

At five o'clock the woman opens the paper. It says, "Before five o'clock, you will write no on this paper." Well, by writing no, the swami caused the event written on the paper to happen, which made his prediction wrong. Would he have predicted correctly if he had written yes? No, because then he would have been predicting that he would write no. There was no way that the swami could have been correct, no matter what he wrote!

RIDDLES, PUZZLES, AND MATH MAGIC

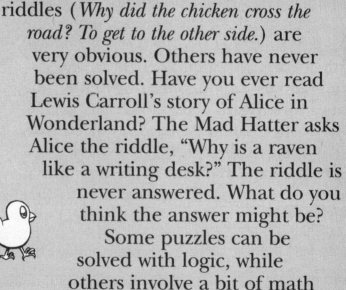

Throughout the ages, we humans have taken great delight in posing questions and problems to confound, confuse, mystify, and baffle each other. Some riddles (*Why did the chicken cross the road? To get to the other side.*) are very obvious. Others have never been solved. Have you ever read Lewis Carroll's story of Alice in Wonderland? The Mad Hatter asks Alice the riddle, "Why is a raven like a writing desk?" The riddle is never answered. What do you think the answer might be? Some puzzles can be solved with logic, while others involve a bit of math wizardry. Sharpen your pencil, muster your mental powers, and tackle the following collection of brain teasers. Then try them on your friends!

When you multiply 9 by any other number, the sum of the digits in the answer always adds up to 9.
Try it!

$9 \times 347 = 3123$ $3 + 1 + 2 + 3 = 9$

SQUARE MATH

Here is a foolproof way to amaze your friends. First, write the number 34 on a piece of paper without letting anyone see what you have written, then place the paper inside an envelope and seal it. Have a friend write down the numbers 1 through 16 in a square like this:

1	2	3	4
5	6	7	8
9	10	11	12
13	14	15	16

Then ask your friend to follow these steps:

1 Circle any number, then cross off all other numbers in the horizontal row and vertical column the circled number is in.

2 Repeat this process for another number and then a third number.

3 Circle the only number that is left over.

4 Tell your friend that you know the sum of the four circled numbers and that the answer is in the sealed envelope.

The sum will always be 34, no matter which numbers are circled.

(You don't believe it? Look on page 64!)

How many balls of string does it take to reach the moon?

(One, if it's long enough!)

Drive Your Friends to Distraction!

Here's a riddle to ask a friend. Say it just like this:

You're driving a bus into town, and at the first stop, ten people get on the bus. At the next stop, four people get on and three get off. At the third stop, two people get on and seven get off. What color are the bus driver's eyes?
(Turn to page 64 for the answer.)

APPLES AND ORANGES

Let's say you have three boxes of fruit. One is labeled Apples, another is labeled Oranges, and the last box is labeled Apples and Oranges. But (you might have guessed) all of the labels are incorrect. Without looking into the boxes, how is it possible to switch the labels so they are correct by taking only one piece of fruit from one of the boxes?
(Go to page 64 to find out how.)

AND THE WINNER IS . . .

A very wealthy man had two sons. The boys had two things in common. They were both excellent horsemen, and they both wanted to inherit their father's estate. One day the man told his quarreling children that his heir would be chosen in a most unusual way. Upon his death, his sons must compete against each other in a horse race, and the son whose horse *lost* the race would inherit the family fortune. How is it possible to run a race in which both competitors are trying to lose?
(See page 64 for the answer.)

ONE BY ONE

Multiplying numbers made up of ones can produce a bit of odd but true math magic:

$$11 \times 11 = 121$$
$$111 \times 111 = 12{,}321$$
$$1{,}111 \times 1{,}111 = 1{,}234{,}321$$
$$11{,}111 \times 11{,}111 = 123{,}454{,}321$$
$$111{,}111 \times 111{,}111 = 12{,}345{,}654{,}321$$
$$1{,}111{,}111 \times 1{,}111{,}111 = 1{,}234{,}567{,}654{,}321$$
$$11{,}111{,}111 \times 11{,}111{,}111 = 123{,}456{,}787{,}654{,}321$$
$$111{,}111{,}111 \times 111{,}111{,}111 = 12{,}345{,}678{,}987{,}654{,}321$$

LOOK, MA, NO HANDS!

How can you lift an ice cube out of a glass of water with nothing but a little salt and a piece of string (and without touching the ice cube with your hands)? You can't tie the string to the ice cube, because you would have to touch it with your hands to do that. Here's where a little scientific know-how can help you fool your friends.

To do this trick, rest the end of the string on top of the ice cube, then sprinkle it with salt. The salt temporarily lowers the freezing point of water, so the ice melts a bit, then refreezes, trapping the string. You can then lift the ice cube out of the water because it is frozen to the end of the string!

HAPPY BIRTHDAY!

You can guess anyone's exact birth date by having that person follow the instructions below. (The birth date of **March 12, 1982,** has been used as an example.)

1 Ask the person to write down the number of his or her month of birth (with January being number 1 and so on).
(March = 3)

2 Add this to the number that comes after the number he or she has just written down.
(3 + 4 = 7)

3 Multiply by 5.
(7 x 5 = 35)

4 Put zero at the end of the total.
(35 becomes 350)

5 Add any one- or two-digit number. (Ask the person to tell you what number he or she added.)
(If he or she picked 77, for example, 350 + 77 = 427)

6 Add the day of the month he or she was born.
(427 + 12 = 439)

7 Pick any one- or two-digit number and write it at the end of the current total. (Ask the person to tell you what number he or she chose.)
(If he or she picked 43, for example, 439 becomes 43943)

8 Add the last two numbers of the year of his or her birth.
(43943 + 82 = 44025)

9 Have your friend tell you his or her total.

While your friend is following your instructions, add 50 to the number he or she randomly picked in step 5.
(50 + 77 = 127)

Place the number he or she randomly picked in step 7 at the end of the above number.
(12743)

Now deduct the above number from the total in step 8.
(44025 − 12743 = 31282)

The answer is his or her birth date . . .
3-12-82!

(Note: If there is a zero in the answer, the dash goes to the right of the zero, as in 10-20-82.)

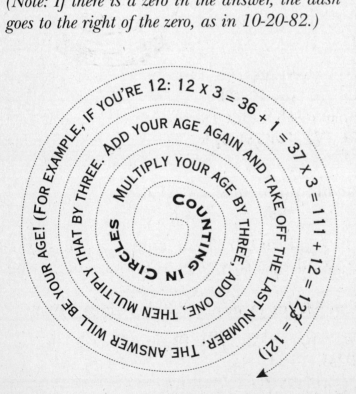

COUNTING IN CIRCLES

MULTIPLY YOUR AGE BY THREE, ADD ONE, THEN MULTIPLY THAT BY THREE. ADD YOUR AGE AGAIN AND TAKE OFF THE LAST NUMBER. THE ANSWER WILL BE YOUR AGE! (FOR EXAMPLE, IF YOU'RE 12: 12 X 3 = 36 + 1 = 37 X 3 = 111 + 12 = 12¾ = 12!)

CALENDAR CUNNING

This one might look tricky, but it's easy. Ask a friend to add up a set of numbers without showing them to you, and you can predict the total. In fact, you can write down the total before you even begin the trick! Follow the example below to learn how it's done. (Assume the current year is 1995, but the trick works for any year.)

1 Have your friend write down the year of his or her birth.
(For example, **1983**)

2 The next number is a year in which something very important happened to your friend.
(Your friend chooses **1987**, the year your friend's brother was born)

3 Next is your friend's age at the end of the present year.
(At the end of 1995, your friend will be **12**)

4 The final entry is the number of years since his or her special event.
(1987 to 1995 = **8**)

These numbers all add up to 3990.
(1983 + 1987 + 12 + 8 = **3990**)

Meanwhile, all you have to do is multiply the current year by 2 (1995 x 2 = **3990**). It will always work out because your friend's birth year and age at the end of the year add up to the current year (1983 + 12 = **1995**). The special event and the number of years since that event will also add up to the current year (1987 + 8 = **1995**). So, by multiplying the current year by 2, you'll always predict the correct answer.

MEASURE FOR MEASURE

A lemonade recipe calls for 4 ounces of lemon juice, but you have only a large, unmarked bottle of juice, a 5-ounce container, and a 3-ounce container. How can you measure out exactly 4 ounces?

1 Begin by filling the 5-ounce container with lemon juice.

2 Next, fill the 3-ounce container from the 5-ounce container (leaving 2 ounces behind), then pour the juice from the 3-ounce container back into the bottle.

3 Pour the 2 ounces of lemon juice from the 5-ounce container into the empty 3-ounce container. You now have a 3-ounce container with 2 ounces of lemon juice in it. You also have an empty 5-ounce container.

4 Fill the 5-ounce container with juice from the bottle and pour enough juice (an ounce) from the 5-ounce container into the 3-ounce container to fill it. You now have a full 3-ounce container, and a 5-ounce container that is holding exactly 4 ounces of juice!

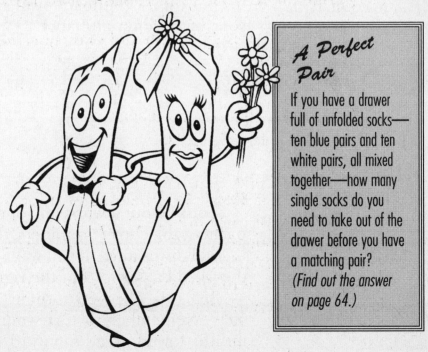

A Perfect Pair

If you have a drawer full of unfolded socks—ten blue pairs and ten white pairs, all mixed together—how many single socks do you need to take out of the drawer before you have a matching pair? *(Find out the answer on page 64.)*

BOOK BITES

Suppose you have a set of three books standing side by side on your bookshelf. Each volume is 2 inches thick. Now imagine a hungry bookworm eating its way from the first page of volume one to the last page of volume three. How many inches does it gobble through?

(Go to page 64 to find out.)

(Go to page 64 to find out.)

Look at the sentence "Railroad crossings without any cars." Can you spell it without any R's?

(See answer on page 64.)

AN ADDED WORD

Did you know that you can spell out words on a pocket calculator?

Punch in the number 5663 on your calculator, then turn it upside down. You'll find the word **EGGS** in the display window. Read on to find out how to make up words of your own. Use the following numbers as your seven-letter alphabet:

$$0 = O$$
$$1 = I$$
$$3 = E$$
$$4 = H$$
$$5 = S$$
$$6 = G$$
$$7 = L$$

To spell out a word on your calculator, pick out the correct numbers, then reverse them. For instance, if you want to spell out the word **LESS**, pick out the right numbers —7355—then reverse them and enter 5537. Remember to turn your calculator upside down to read the word.

GOING UP?

Ms. James works on the 40th floor of her office building. Every morning she arrives at work before anyone else. She rides the elevator alone to the 30th floor, then she gets off and walks the rest of the way. At night, she rides all the way down. Why? *(Find out on page 64.)*

SMALL CHANGE

If your parents asked you to do the dishes for one month and offered to pay you 1¢ per day, but also offered to double your pay each day, would it be worth it? *(Answer is on page 64.)*

TONGUE TWISTERS

Do you and your friends need a few laughs? Try saying each of these tongue twisters out loud three times in a row, as fast as you can.

Silly Caesar seized his knees and sneezed.

Precious Polly playfully picked pretty pink pansies.

Two tough trucks took ten twins to town.

The sixth sick sheik's sixth sheep's sick.

APPEARANCES ARE DECEIVING
OPTICAL ILLUSIONS

Have you ever heard the saying, "I'll believe it when I see it with my own eyes"? But your eyes can play tricks on you! An optical illusion is an image that is in some way misleading and may cause you to draw the wrong conclusions. In other words, an optical illusion can fool your brain into thinking you are seeing something that might not actually be there. Here are a few illusions for you to ponder.

THE MAN IN THE MOON

Have you ever looked up at a full Moon and noticed that it appears to be looking back at you? What looks like the eyes, nose, and open mouth of this lunar lad is really just shadow play. The highlands of the Moon block sunlight from falling on its large lowland areas, called *maria*, or "seas." These dark lowland areas are what we interpret as the crude features of a face.

MOON MAGIC

When a full Moon rises over the horizon, it usually looks larger than when it is high in the sky, but (of course) its actual size is always the same. That's because, when the Moon is on the horizon, you can compare it to objects such as trees or houses, so your brain interprets it as being fairly large. When the Moon is high in the sky, you don't have anything to compare the Moon to, so it appears smaller.

18

DEFYING GRAVITY

Here's a little trick that you can do to impress your friends. You'll need two books of different thicknesses (one about 1 inch thick, the other at least twice as thick), two yardsticks, two funnels of the same size, and masking tape.

1 Tape the wide ends of the funnels together (A).

2 Put the books down flat, a little less than 3 feet apart, and balance the yardsticks on them so that the opening between them is narrow at the end with the thin book and wide at the end with the thick book.

3 Place the funnels at the narrow end. They will now appear to roll uphill! In fact, the funnels are rolling down from (or lower than) the spot where they started. To prove this, take a look at the position of the spouts of the funnels relative to the yardsticks (B). You will see that at the high end of the yardsticks, the spouts are actually lower than where they started. Because the track itself is tilted upward, it gives the illusion that the funnels are rolling uphill.

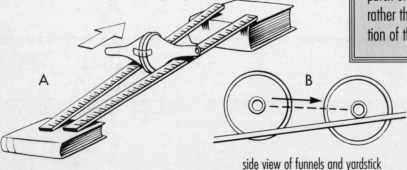

side view of funnels and yardstick

A HANDY TRICK

Did you know there is a large hole in the center of your hand? Well, you can at least see the illusion of one! Put the open end of a cardboard tube (a paper towel roll tube is ideal) up to your right eye. Hold your left hand next to the tube (at about the middle of the tube), with your open palm facing you. Now, with both eyes open, stare at a spot in the distance. You will notice that there is a perfect hole in the middle of your hand. It appears because your brain combines the images seen by each eye into one.

THE PHANTOM FINGER

Here's a variation of the illusion created in "A Handy Trick." Hold your hands up at eye level about a foot or so from your face. Now point your two index fingers at each other about an inch apart and stare at a distant spot. You will see a stubby little finger suspended between your index fingers!

*P*lace a pencil in the center of a glass of water and look at it from the side. The pencil appears to be broken (shifted) where it enters the water.

OPTICAL ILLUSIONS

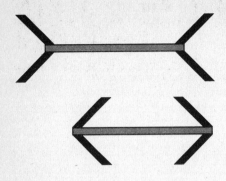

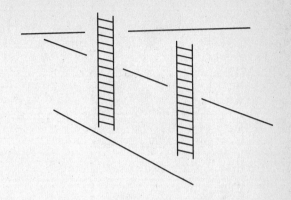

Which gray line is longer?

(Although the top line may appear longer, the two lines are actually the same length.)

Which ladder is taller?

(The two ladders are the same height.)

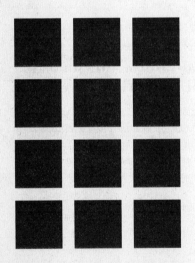

Stare at these squares for at least ten seconds. Do you see anything else?

(You will see fuzzy gray dots just outside the corners of each square, or lines running between the squares.)

Are the horizontal rows in this drawing straight, or do they slope upward?

(They're straight, and if you don't believe it, a ruler will prove it to you!)

Is this a picture of an old woman or a young woman?

(That depends upon whether you see the eye, nose, mouth, and chin of a woman facing toward the left and slightly down, or the ear, chin, and neck of a woman with her face turned to the left and away from you.)

Here is a picture of an animal. But what animal do you see?

(You can see a rabbit facing toward the right or a duck facing toward the left.)

Look carefully. This picture could fool you. What do you see?

(It's a man or a mouse! Need a hint? The round circles at the top of the drawing can be the glasses of an old man or the ears of a mouse.)

It's easy to see what is represented here. Or is it?

(Depending on what you concentrate on, you can see two people in white silhouette talking or a black vase.)

IS THIS FOR REAL?

LOONY LAWS, STRANGE FACTS, AND CURIOUS CUSTOMS

■ ■ ■ ■ ■ ■ ■ ■ ■ ■ ■ ■ ■ ■ ■

Did you know that in New York it is illegal to open an umbrella in front of a horse? Or that in 1471 a chicken was burned at the stake in Basel, Switzerland, for laying a strangely colored egg? Or that the Silbo language of the Canary Islanders is made up solely of whistles?

Here is a collection of loony laws, strange facts, and unusual customs from around the world that you won't believe are for real!

LOONY LAWS

✹ In Idaho, you can't give an individual a box of candy that weighs more than 50 pounds.

✹ In Alaska, it is illegal to look at a moose from a moving aircraft.

▸···········
In Kentucky, you are required by law to take a bath at least once a year.
···········◂

Guess what is against the law in the landlocked state of Oklahoma? Catching whales!

✸ There is an old law still on the books in Kentucky that makes it illegal for a married man to buy a hat without his wife along to help him pick it out.

✸ It's against the law in Texas to milk someone else's cow unless you have permission.

✸ In Oklahoma, it is against the law to give alcohol to fish.

✸ In Dunn, North Carolina, there is an ordinance that forbids people to snore loudly enough to disturb their neighbors. The penalty is a night or two in jail.

✸ A sow was hanged in France in 1547 for causing the death of a child. Her six piglets were excused from punishment because they were too young to know better and their mother had set such a bad example.

✸ In Turkey, during the 16th and 17th centuries, you could be put to death for drinking coffee.

✸ It's against the law to slurp your soup in New Jersey.

WATCH YOUR STEP

By law, you may not blow your nose in public or walk down the street with your shoelaces untied in Maine.

In 1499, lawyers for a bear on trial in Germany argued that it should be tried by a jury of its peers, which, of course, meant a jury of bears. Their request was turned down.

NOT GUILTY

✱ If you have smelly feet, you are not allowed to remove your shoes in a public theater in Winnetka, Illinois. Similarly, in Gary, Indiana, you cannot enter a theater within four hours of eating garlic.

✱ In Memphis, Tennessee, it is illegal for frogs to croak after 11 P.M.

✱ To buy ice cream after 6 P.M. in Newark, New Jersey, you are supposed to have a note from your doctor.

STRANGE FACTS

How much blood do you have? Divide your weight by 12 to find out how many pints course through your veins.

BLOOD BY ANY OTHER COLOR . . .

What color is blood? Within the body it may be red or blue. Oxygen-rich blood in the arteries is red. Oxygen-poor blood in the veins is blue. When you cut open a vein, however, the blood immediately reacts with the oxygen in the air and flows as red.

BODY FACTS

➪ Your hair contains about 430 parts per million of gold.

➪ You will probably shed about 40 pounds of skin in your lifetime.

➪ When you sneeze, you expel air at about 100 miles per hour. That qualifies as hurricane force!

➪ It takes 17 muscles to smile and 43 to frown.

➪ If you placed all of the blood vessels of your body end to end, they would stretch around the Earth $2\frac{1}{2}$ times!

➪ Blood is six times thicker than water.

AMAGING ANIMALS

- A jellyfish can still sting you after it is dead. One scientist found this out the hard way. He performed an experiment using chopped-up jellyfish tentacles, then, several months later, he happened to wear the same lab coat that he had used during the experiment. When he accidentally got the sleeve of the coat wet, he was stung several times on his wrist!

A *jellyfish is made up of about 95 percent water.*

- Have you ever heard of a fish in the desert? The Devil's Hole pup-fish lives in a small pool that is only 50 feet long, 10 feet wide, and about 60 feet deep. It can survive water temperatures as hot as 120 degrees Fahrenheit.

- An 18-foot-tall giraffe and a 4-inch-long field mouse have the same number of neck vertebrae (seven). Those of the giraffe, obviously, are much longer.

Ostriches have the odd habit of swallowing shiny things. In South Africa, one ostrich was found to have swallowed 53 diamonds!

27

Porcupines love salt. They have been known to munch on the wooden handles of shovels that have absorbed salty perspiration from human hands. One porcupine reportedly gnawed the wooden steering wheel of a forest ranger's car!

A Porpoise with a Purpose

In New Zealand, there is a treacherous water passage known as French Pass, which leads from Pelorus Sound to Tasman Bay. It has dangerous rocks and unpredictable currents. In 1871, during a storm, the crew of an American schooner noted a playful porpoise at the bow. They followed the porpoise, which led them safely through deep water. From that time on, for 40 years, that same porpoise, known as Pelorus Jack, guided hundreds of ships through the dangerous pass.

- In just 12 minutes, a mole can dig a tunnel 6½ feet long.

- In England in the late 1400s, King Richard III sentenced a court noble, Sir Henry Wyat, to death by starvation. Wyat was locked up in the Tower of London to die. Wyat's faithful cat, however, followed him and was able to slip in and out of the prison through a chimney. Each day it would catch a pigeon for Wyat to eat. When, after several months, the nobleman was still alive, King Richard investigated and was so impressed by the loyalty of the cat that he pardoned Wyat.

- Hummingbirds' wings move so fast that they are almost invisible. Some hummingbirds beat their wings as fast as 4,500 times per minute! And, unlike any other bird, they can fly backward, sideways, and even upside down.

FLOWING FEATS AND OTHER NATURAL WONDERS

✪ In some places along the coast of New Zealand, waterfalls tumbling over the steep coastal cliffs never reach the ground. The ocean wind is so powerful that the falling water is blown back *up*.

✪ The extremely high tides of the Bay of Fundy in Canada cause an amazing event—a reversing waterfall! As the St. John River flows into the Bay of Fundy, it must pass through a very narrow gorge. When the tide rises in the bay, water builds up very high at the mouth of the gorge and pours into the river. This creates a waterfall until the level of the river rises. As the tide retreats, the water level becomes higher on the opposite side of the gorge. Then, the thundering waterfall returns, but it falls in the other direction!

If all the oceans in the world were to dry up, they would leave behind enough salt to build a wall around Earth's equator 1 mile thick and 18 miles high.

*N*iagara Falls is retreating upriver because the rushing waters are wearing the underlying cliff away. In about 23,000 years, the falls will disappear altogether.

✪ You've probably heard the saying "raining cats and dogs," but how about raining fish and frogs? On October 23, 1947, it rained in Marsville, Louisiana, but along with the large raindrops that fell from the sky, a large number of fish fell as well. Some of the fish were as much as 9 inches long! And on June 16, 1882, the people of Dubuque, Iowa, were pelted with hailstones with tiny frogs trapped inside. How did it happen? Not by magic. These animals were probably drawn into the clouds from nearby streams and ponds by strong updrafts or even tornadoes.

✪ Because of the extreme cold and the high concentration of ultraviolet rays, there are few if any bacteria on Antarctica. For that reason, food doesn't spoil. Food left behind 80 years ago by early explorers has been found still in edible condition.

✪ About 32 billion pounds of snow and rain fall to Earth *every second!*

*L*ightning bolts may reach temperatures five times hotter than the surface of the sun. Lightning has even been known to melt the nails in a building and to cook potatoes growing in fields.

✿ Tornadoes do not always cause destruction. A tornado in Italy lifted a sleeping baby in its carriage 50 feet up into the air and then set it gently down more than 300 feet away. The baby was not only unharmed, it didn't even wake up!

WILD BLUE YONDER

In 1959, due to an emergency, a pilot bailed out of his plane at 47,000 feet into a huge thundercloud. It should have taken only 10 minutes for him to float gently to Earth with his parachute, but he didn't fall. Instead, he was tossed up and down and was rolled and slammed by the violent gusts inside the cloud (these gusts can reach speeds of up to 65 miles per hour). There was so much water in the cloud, he could barely breathe and feared that he might drown. By the time he made it safely to the ground, he had spent 40 terrifying minutes in the heart of the black cloud.

✿ You'll never be able to find a pot of gold at the end of a rainbow. That's because a rainbow has no end! It is actually a circle. You see it as a half circle because the horizon cuts off the rainbow's other half from view. From an airplane, you would be able to see the entire ring.

SPACE FACTS

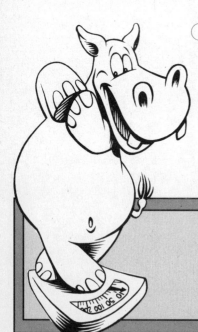

● The Moon is moving away from Earth at about half an inch a year. When the Moon first formed it was probably half the distance from Earth that it is now—about 135,000 miles.

◐ The Moon's gravity affects the waters of Earth, causing them to bulge upward. We see this effect in the form of tides. The planet Jupiter has a similar, but much stronger, effect on its moon, Io. The gravitational attraction of Jupiter causes the land surface of Io to bulge upward by about 300 feet.

◑ A space vehicle must reach a speed of 7 miles per second to escape Earth's gravity. An airplane flying that fast would travel from New York City to Philadelphia in 20 seconds!

○ When you look out into space, you are actually looking back into the past. It takes about 2 million years for light from the farthest object visible to the naked eye to reach Earth, so we are seeing that object (the Andromeda Galaxy) as it looked 2 million years ago.

> ## It's a Bird, It's a Plane, It's...
>
> Earth moves in orbit around the Sun at a speed approximately eight times that of a speeding bullet.

LOST (POUNDS, THAT IS) IN SPACE

If you weigh 100 pounds on Earth, you would weigh 38 pounds on Mercury.

MATH FOR MOTHER NATURE

⇨ To estimate the distance of a storm, count the number of seconds that elapse between a flash of lightning and the sound of thunder, then divide by 5. The result is how many miles away the storm is.

⇨ You can tell how fast waves are moving onto shore by counting the seconds between two arriving crests, then multiplying by 3½. The resulting number is the speed of the oncoming waves in miles per hour.

⇨ To figure out the temperature outdoors, time the chirps of a cricket. Count the number of chirps in 15 seconds and add 37. It will be quite close to the Fahrenheit temperature. (This only works in warm weather, though.)

In 1868, about 100,000 tiny meteorites fell on the city of Pultusk, Poland, in one night.

STRANGER STILL

☛ Contrary to popular belief, Paul Revere was not alone on his famous ride at the beginning of the American Revolution. On April 18, 1775, Revere and a cobbler named William Dawes both took to the saddle to warn the colonists that the British were about to attack. Once Lexington had been warned, another man, Samuel Prescott, joined the others on the journey to Concord. The three were chased by British soldiers and had to split up. Dawes returned to Lexington. Revere was stopped by the British and sent back to Lexington on foot. Only Prescott made it to Concord.

One . . .
Two . . .
Three . . .
How long would it take you to count up to one billion at the rate of one number per second? About 32 years!

A *ten-gallon hat can actually hold only about 3 quarts of water.*

☞ In 1895, there were only two automobiles in the entire state of Ohio that were regularly driven on the roads. Somehow, the drivers still managed to crash into each other!

GHOST SHIP

In 1906, Norwegian explorer Roald Amundsen took three years to sail from the Atlantic Ocean to the Pacific Ocean by a northern route. He was the first to successfully complete the dangerous passage through the ice-choked Arctic Ocean—the first, that is, to do it *alive*.

One hundred and thirty-one years before, in August 1775, a lookout on the whaling ship *Herald* spotted an apparently deserted, drifting schooner—the *Octavius*—off the west coast of Greenland. When a small party boarded the *Octavius*, they were horrified at the ship's dreadful cargo: the well-preserved bodies of the captain and his wife, the first mate, 28 crew members, and a cabin boy. All had frozen to death. Upon examining the ship's log, the captain of the *Herald* discovered that the *Octavius* had become trapped in the ice of the frigid ocean near Point Barrow, Alaska—about a thousand miles to the west! The last entry was dated November 11, 1762, so, in fact, the *Octavius* was the first ship known to travel a northern passage from the Pacific Ocean to the Atlantic Ocean. It made the voyage slowly over 13 years, with a crew of corpses.

☞ The spark that set off World War I was the assassination of Archduke Franz Ferdinand and his wife in Sarajevo, Bosnia, on June 28, 1914. They were shot while riding in a bright red Phaeton car. From that time on, anyone who owned that vehicle suffered misfortune. Over the next 10 years or so, the car was involved in accidents resulting in the deaths of a total of 16 persons. It was restored and placed on exhibit in a museum in Vienna, where it finally met its end when a bomb destroyed the museum during World War II.

In the original French folktale, Cinderella's slippers were not made of glass. There was a mistake made when the story was finally written down in 1697 for *The Tales of Mother Goose (Contes de Ma Mère L'oye)*. The folktale originally had Cinderella wearing slippers of *vair,* or "white squirrel fur." The translator thought it was the word *verre,* which sounds the same but means "glass."

CURIOUS CUSTOMS

Customs are different from one place to another. In Japan, it is considered lucky to spill salt. Also, when in mourning, the Japanese wear white.

⊕ In some parts of Great Britain, when people move, it is the custom to use hot embers from their old home to light a fire in the hearth of their new home. This is probably the origin of the term *housewarming.*

⊕ On the island of Malta, in the Mediterranean Sea, churches have two clock faces. One shows the correct time, while the other is incorrect. This is to confuse the Devil so he won't make it to services on time.

⊕ The ancient Egyptians honored a beloved cat by mummifying its remains. They must have certainly admired cats, because thousands of cat mummies have been discovered. Strangely, a similar number of mouse mummies have been found as well, even though Egyptians were not known to have revered mice. So what explains the mouse mummies? They were probably mummified to provide food for the *cat* on its journey to the next life!

*7*he ancient Egyptians also prized (of all things!) the onion. They thought it kept evil spirits away. They so believed in its powers that people took an oath to tell the truth on an onion, just as we do on the Bible in court today.

To superstitious people, walking under a ladder is considered bad luck. But many believe you can counteract the misfortune by keeping your fingers crossed until you see a dog.

TAKE TWO PIGEONS AND CALL ME IN THE MORNING

The Black Plague raged throughout Europe during the 1300s and killed thousands of people. A number of unusual remedies were suggested to avoid catching the dreaded disease. People were advised to:

➭ Ring bells and shoot off cannons and muskets to break up the plague vapors.

➭ Bring spiders into the house so their webs would absorb the plague vapors.

➭ Bathe in goat urine.

➭ Place dried toads over a plague victim's boils.

➭ Place the internal organs of a young pigeon on a plague victim's forehead.

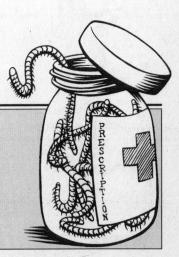

In England, during the time of King Charles II, doctors thought that brushing the inside of the stomach would keep one healthy. They told their patients to do this by swallowing 50 or more wiggly-legged millipedes each day.

FROM ONE EXTREME TO THE OTHER

Our planet is a place of extremes, from the scorching heat of the Sahara to the bitter cold of Antarctica. And take trees. Some tower more than 20 stories into the air, while others are so tiny that a small child can step over them.

On the following pages, you will learn a lot more of these amazing comparisons—the biggest and smallest, the longest and shortest, the fastest and slowest —from one extreme to the other.

THE LIVING WORLD

☞ Can you imagine an animal as big and heavy as a dump truck? The African elephant, the **largest land-dwelling mammal** on Earth, fits that description. The biggest one on record was an astonishing 25 feet long from trunk to tail and 13 feet high at the shoulder, and weighed more than 20,000 pounds.

The **world's smallest land-dwelling mammal** might easily go unnoticed as it scurries through the grasslands of Africa or Asia. The Savi's pygmy shrew, which is about 2 inches long and weighs 0.07 ounces, is so tiny that it can crawl into a hole made by an earthworm!

☞ If you look on the back of a one-dollar bill, you will find a picture of a bald eagle, a well-known symbol of the United States. This remarkable bird is also known as the **builder of the largest bird nest**. The biggest bald-eagle nest found was 9 feet in diameter and 20 feet deep, and weighed about 6,700 pounds. You could stretch out very comfortably in such a roomy nest.

You would barely be able to find room for your toe in the thimble-sized nest of the Cuban bee hummingbird. The tiny home—the **world's smallest nest**—is usually less than an inch in diameter and in depth, and weighs only a fraction of an ounce.

☞ The **world's slowest mammal** is the three-toed sloth of South America. It creeps along (when it moves at all) at no more than 0.15 miles per hour. At that rate, it would take a sloth more than 20 minutes to "race" down a football field from one goalpost to the other.

At top speed, the cheetah of Africa would cover the length of the same football field in about 3½ seconds! The cheetah is the **world's fastest mammal**. It can reach running speeds of 60 to 65 miles per hour.

☞ It is possible that a Seychelles tortoise living today hatched from its egg in the mid-1800s, before the U.S. Civil War began. This huge tortoise **lives longer than any other animal**—the greatest verified age for one of these creatures is 156 years.

The creature with the **shortest life span** can measure its time on Earth with a clock rather than a calendar. The adult mayfly may live for as little as two hours.

☞ High up in the Himalayas, the world's tallest mountain range, you'll find plenty of snow and ice. You'll also find the **mammal that lives at the highest altitude** — a large member of the ox family known as the Tibetan yak. It may forage for food in areas as high as 20,000 feet up in the mountains.

The **mammal that makes its home at the greatest depth** in the Earth is the little brown bat. Colonies of this bat have been found in mines as deep as 3,500 feet.

You might not be too pleased to get a bouquet of the **world's largest flower**—the rafflesia—because it is reported to smell somewhat like rotting meat! The rafflesia, which grows in Borneo, has no roots or leaves, but its flower is 3 feet across and weighs up to 15 pounds.

The **world's smallest flower** is on the world's smallest flowering plant, a Brazilian duckweed called *wolffia*. The plant itself is no more than 1/16 inch across, and its flower is half that size.

☞ The living world contains many giant and midget plants, too. The **most massive tree** is the General Sherman, a *sequoia gigantia* in Sequoia National Park in California. It is about 272 feet tall and approximately 100 feet in circumference at its base, and is estimated to weigh more than 4 million pounds. The **world's tallest trees** are the redwoods of California, the *sequoia sempervirens*. The tallest—the Howard Libbey tree in Redwood Creek Grove in Humboldt County—is 366 feet tall.

The **world's smallest trees** grow on the Arctic tundra. They are dwarf willows that are only about 2 inches tall.

When you think of a giant animal, a frog may not be the first creature that comes to mind, but the Goliath frog of Africa really measures up. The **world's biggest frog**, the Goliath is 3 feet long from the tip of its snout to the end of its back and may weigh as much as 10 pounds.

*The **world's smallest frog** is found in Cuba. It is* Sminthillus limbatus, *which is only about half an inch long.*

PLANET EARTH

Earth is often called the blue planet because it is covered mostly by water. Oceans blanket about 75 percent of the planet. The **largest and deepest ocean** of all is the Pacific Ocean, which is 64,186,300 square miles in size and 35,810 feet deep at its deepest point.

The **smallest, shallowest ocean** is the Arctic, at 2,966,000 square miles and only 17,880 feet deep.

Cherrapunji, India, is considered one of the **wettest places on Earth.** In a single year— from August 1860 to August 1861—a record 1,042 inches of rain fell. The **most rain in one 24-hour period** fell on Cilaos, La Reunion, in the Indian Ocean. That small town was pelted with 73.62 inches of rain in one day.

They could use a little of that rain in the Atacama Desert of Chile, where the town of Calama has had only one rainfall in the past 400 years. That makes it the **driest place on Earth.**

There are two rivers that contend for the title of the **world's longest river.** The Nile in Africa is reported to be 4,145 miles in length from its recognized source to its outlet into the Mediterranean Sea. Seasonal changes and flooding make it difficult to define the exact source and accurately measure the length of the Amazon in South America. Some scientists claim that this river is also about 4,145 miles in length, while others believe it to be about 4,195 miles from its source to its outlet into the Atlantic Ocean, making *it* the world's longest river.

There's no competition for the title of the **world's shortest river.** It's the Roe River in Montana, and it flows only 201 feet before it joins the Missouri River.

The average air temperature on Earth is around 70 degrees Fahrenheit. The **highest air temperature on record** was nearly double that—134.6 degrees! It was recorded at Azizia in Libya.

The **lowest temperature,** a shivery –129 degrees Fahrenheit, was recorded at Vostok Station, a Russian research station in Antarctica.

High and Low

The **highest point on land** is Mount Everest in Nepal. It is 29,028 feet above sea level. However, this record has been challenged by some who believe another Himalayan peak called K2 is slightly higher.

The **lowest point on land** is the area of the Dead Sea in Jordan. There, the land dips to 1,302 feet below sea level. The Dead Sea is also the **world's lowest-level navigable lake.** The **highest navigable lake** is Lake Titicaca in Peru, at 12,506 feet above sea level.

A WORD ABOUT WORDS

 The **language with the largest vocabulary** is English. It includes about 800,000 words and technical terms.

The **language with the smallest vocabulary** is Taki Taki, spoken in an area of French Guinea, South America. It has no technical terms and only 340 words.

 The **alphabet with the most letters** is the Cambodian alphabet, with 72.

The **alphabet with the least letters** is a language of the South Pacific called Rotokas. It has 11 letters.

A LEAGUE OF THEIR OWN

■ ■ ■ ■ ■ ■ ■ ■ ■ ■ ■ ■ ■ ■ ■

Our world is filled with standouts of every description. For example, the largest crocodile ever was *Deinosuchus* (dine-oh-SOOK-us). It lived more than 65 million years ago in what is now Texas, and grew to be over 52 feet long!

And no matter what the category, someone or something was always the first. Did you know that the first speeding ticket was given in 1904 in Newport, Rhode Island? The driver was going 5 miles faster than the 15-mile-per-hour speed limit and was sentenced to one day in jail for each mile over the limit.

Some things stand out because there is nothing else like them. For example, the one and only marsupial (pouched mammal) native to North America is the Virginia opossum.

So here are the stars—the record holders, the famous firsts, and the one-of-a-kinds that belong in a category all their own.

RECORD HOLDERS

☆ You don't have to see the African zorilla (also called the striped polecat) to know that it is nearby. It is the world's smelliest animal. This relative of the skunk sprays a fluid that can be detected by humans up to a mile away!

SPEED DEMONS

Fastest bird in a dive	Peregrine falcon	217 miles per hour
Fastest fish	Sailfish	68 miles per hour
Fastest snake	Black mamba	20 miles per hour
Fastest insect	Dragonfly	36 miles per hour

For its body size, the kiwi lays the largest egg of any bird. The egg is at least one-quarter the size of the parent. That's like a chicken laying an egg the size of a baseball!

☆ Many animals travel in groups such as packs, pods, herds, flocks, or schools. Sometimes the group members can number in the hundreds or even thousands. The largest gathering of animals on record was a swarm of krill (tiny shrimplike sea animals) in Antarctica. The total weight of the billions of creatures in the swarm was estimated to be about 20 billion pounds!

☆ The animal that travels the farthest during migration is the Arctic tern. This amazing bird flies all the way from the North Pole to the South Pole every year. That's a round trip of 25,000 miles!

On record, the cat that lived the longest was a tabby in England. The cat lived to be 36 years old.

Cats hold some other records, too. The heaviest known domestic was an old tomcat from Connecticut that weighed 43 pounds.

✪ The Emperor penguin holds not one but three records! This penguin is the diving champ of the bird world. It can dive to depths of more than 900 feet to catch the squid it likes to eat. The Emperor is also the world's largest penguin. It is about 3½ feet tall and weighs close to 100 pounds. It also holds the record for having the most feathers—280 per square inch, or about 30,000 altogether.

✪ The ocean floor far below the water's surface is a dark, cold place. But life can be found even there. The greatest ocean depth at which a fish has been found alive is 36,000 feet. The crew of the *Trieste*, a deep-sea diving vessel, noted a fish at that depth that seemed to be a type of sole. They also noted other life forms including a Gorgon sea fan (at 20,100 feet), a sea lily (at 27,100 feet), and a sea cucumber (at 33,600 feet).

Leaping Legends

You won't find the world's greatest jumpers on a basketball court. The four-legged jumping champion is the puma. It can leap 23 feet up from a standstill and 60 feet down to the ground from a height.

The average flea, which is about $\frac{1}{16}$ of an inch long, can jump 10 inches high (160 times its size) and 14 inches forward (220 times its size). To equal such a jump, a 6-foot, 5-inch-tall person would have to leap about as high as a 90-story skyscraper and as far as the length of four football fields!

BODY PARTS

Longest horns	Water buffalo	13 feet
Longest beak	Australian pelican	20 inches
Longest tongue	Giant anteater	2 feet
Widest wingspan	Wandering albatross	12 feet
Heaviest brain	Sperm whale	about 17 pounds
Longest teeth (tusks)	African elephant	up to 11 feet long

CREEPY CRAWLERS

➪ The Goliath beetle of Africa is the world's heaviest insect. As big as your hand, it weighs 3½ ounces!

➪ The largest spider has a leg span of 10 inches and a body length of 3½ inches. Oh, and it sometimes eats birds. That's why it's called the South American bird-eating spider!

➪ The insect with the longest antennae is *Batocera kibleri*, a 3½-inch-long beetle with 9-inch-long antennae.

➪ The creature with the most legs is certainly the millipede. It has as many as 700 short, wiggly legs!

The world's largest baby, that of the blue whale, is 23 feet long and weighs 4,000 pounds at birth.

☆ There are plenty of record holders in the ocean. For example, the biggest fish is the whale shark, at about 40 feet in length. This seagoing giant also produces the world's largest fish egg. It is 15 inches long and 12 inches wide, and looks more like a leathery case than an egg. In fact, the nickname for this unusual egg (and those of some other sharks) is "mermaid's purse."

☆ The giant squid's claim to fame is that it has the largest eye of any animal— about 15 inches across. It is also the largest invertebrate (animal without a backbone). It may grow to 55 feet in length and weigh as much as 5,000 pounds.

☆ The world's largest cavern is Lobang Nasip Bagus, which is located in East Malaysia on the shores of the South China Sea. The cavern is more than 2,000 feet long and 1,000 feet wide— long enough to fit seven football fields end to end. It is tall enough to house a 20-story building.

☆ Lake Baikal in Russia is the world's deepest lake. It is nearly a mile deep and holds more water than all of the United States' Great Lakes put together.

☆ Where do you think the strongest earthquake in the U.S. took place? Would you guess Missouri? The quake that shook New Madrid, Missouri, in 1811 was so strong that it caused church bells as far away as Boston and Washington, D.C., to ring!

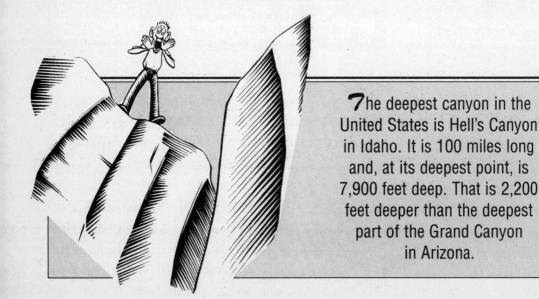

The deepest canyon in the United States is Hell's Canyon in Idaho. It is 100 miles long and, at its deepest point, is 7,900 feet deep. That is 2,200 feet deeper than the deepest part of the Grand Canyon in Arizona.

The world's largest silver nugget was found near Aspen, Colorado, in 1894. It weighed 1,840 pounds.

The largest iceberg was spotted in the Pacific Ocean in 1956. It was 208 miles long and 60 miles wide, or as big as the country of Belgium.

☆ The greatest structure ever built is the Great Wall of China. It is 4,000 miles long and is actually visible from the Moon! Constructed around an inner mound of earth, it is a rock wall 25 feet high and 12 feet thick. The road on top of it can accommodate five horses side by side.

GOING BANANAS

The largest plant without a woody stem is the banana, which can grow to be 30 feet tall. Speaking of bananas, what would you do with 10,000 of them? Make a banana split! The world's largest banana split was put together in 1973 in St. Paul, Minnesota. It included 10,580 bananas and 33,000 scoops of ice cream.

The world's largest ice cream sundae weighed 3,956 pounds. It included 777 gallons of ice cream, 6 gallons of chocolate syrup, a gallon of whipped cream, and a case of chocolate sprinkles.

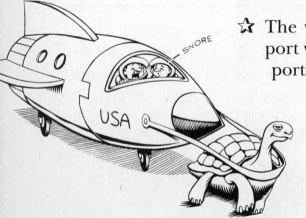
SNORE

USA

☆ The world's largest and slowest transport vehicle is "the Crawler," the transporter that moves the space shuttle to its launch pad at Cape Canaveral. It weighs more than 6 million pounds and plods along at 2 miles per hour. Nevertheless, the driver is still required to wear a seat belt!

The planet with the slowest rotational speed is Mercury. It turns on its axis about as fast as a human can run—6 miles per hour.

☆ The path of the spacecraft *Voyager* was calculated so accurately that it was able to visit four of the five outer planets in the solar system on its journey. That mathematical feat is similar to a golfer making a hole-in-one from 150 miles away.

☆ The planet Mars has the largest known volcano in the solar system. Known as Olympus Mons, it is approximately 300 miles across and 70,000 feet high.

A FINAL WORD

According to the Oxford English Dictionary, the longest commonly used nonmedical term in the English language is *floccipaucinihilipilification*, which means "the act of estimating as worthless." It has 29 letters.

FAMOUS FIRSTS

The very first U.S. coin was a penny minted in 1787. The motto on the coin was not In God We Trust, *but* Mind Your Own Business.

The first man to serve as president in the United States was not George Washington, but a man named John Hanson. Born in 1721, he was elected to the Continental Congress in 1779. Eight months later, he was given the office of president of the Congress of the Confederation. He held the position for a year, during which time his official title was President of the United States in Congress Assembled. Seven other men held that position until 1789, when the Constitution of the United States was ratified. At that time, George Washington was elected as the first official president of the United States.

PRESIDENTIAL FIRSTS

⇨ The first president to live in the White House was John Adams.

⇨ The first president to wear long trousers was Thomas Jefferson.

⇨ Andrew Jackson was the first president to ride on a railroad train.

⇨ Martin Van Buren was the first to be born a citizen of the United States.

⇨ James Garfield was the first to use a telephone.

⇨ Theodore Roosevelt was the first to ride in an automobile and also the first to visit a foreign country while in office (Panama and Puerto Rico).

THE RUN TO WALK FIRST

⇨ The first person to walk in space was Soviet cosmonaut Alexei Leonov, on March 18, 1965. His ship was the *Voskhod 2*.

⇨ The first American to spacewalk was Ed White, on June 3, 1965. His craft was *Gemini 4*.

⇨ Russian Svetlana Savitskava was the first woman to spacewalk, on July 25, 1984. Her ship was *Soyuz T-12*.

⇨ Bruce McCandless was the first to walk in space without a tether, on February 7, 1984. He was part of Shuttle Mission STS-41B.

The first animal inducted into the Animal Hall of Fame was Lassie.

! The first child born in America of European parents was Virginia Dare, on Roanoke Island in 1587.

! The first person born in Antarctica was delivered on an Argentine research base on January 9, 1978.

! The first typewritten (instead of hand-written) manuscript was submitted for publication in 1875. It was *Tom Sawyer* by Mark Twain.

! Nadia Comaneci of Romania was the first Olympic gymnast to score a perfect 10. She accomplished this seven times in the 1976 Olympics when she was only 15.

Calling for Help

The first SOS signal transmitted from a ship in distress was from the *Titanic*.

THE ONE AND ONLY

✪ The sea star (or starfish) is the only animal to take its stomach to its food instead of the other way around! The sea star creeps slowly along until it finds a clam, then uses its strong, gripping arms to force the clam shell open. Then the sea star's stomach bulges out through the creature's mouth, and covers and digests the soft clam.

CURIOUS CONTINENTS

There are no countries on the continent of Antarctica.

There are no deserts on the European continent.

There are no glaciers on the continent of Australia.

The only member of the animal kingdom whose testimony is allowed in a court of law is the bloodhound. Its sense of smell is 1 million times more powerful than that of a human, so if a bloodhound tracks down and so identifies a criminal, that evidence is admissible in court.

AMAZING ANIMALS

◆ **Duck-billed platypus:** the only mammal with a bill

◆ **The bat:** the only mammal that can fly

◆ **Vampire bat:** the only mammal that feeds only on blood

◆ **Nine-banded armadillo:** the only animal to regularly give birth to identical quadruplets

◆ **Naked mole rat:** the only furless rodent

◆ **Maned wolf:** the only member of the dog family that digs with its teeth instead of its claws

◆ **Cheetah:** the only great cat that can't retract its claws

◆ **Sloth bear:** the only bear with no front teeth

◆ **Kakapo:** the only nonflying parrot

◆ **Common-poor-will:** the only hibernating bird

◆ **Burrowing owl:** the only owl to live underground

◆ **Ostrich:** the only two-toed bird

◆ **Sharp-ribbed salamander:** the only animal that uses its ribs as weapons

◆ **Hochstetter's frog:** the only frog with tail-wagging muscles

◆ *Calpe lustrigata* **of Malaysia:** the only moth to drink blood

Lobocraspis griseifusa:
the only moth that drinks tears

★ The only animal known to have a common burial ground is the penguin of South Georgia Island in Antarctica. A scientist once observed sick and injured birds around a hilltop lake. Upon investigation, it turned out that the bottom of the lake was covered with dead penguins preserved by the cold.

INFREQUENT FLYER

The penguin is the only bird that can swim underwater but cannot fly.

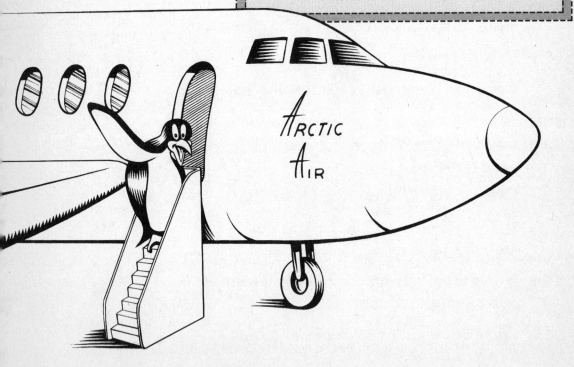

WEIRD WORDS AND FUN PHRASES

Have you ever wondered where a word comes from? Many English words have their roots in other languages, such as Latin or Greek. And you might be surprised by the meanings of the original terms. For example, although some people don't think that politicians are particularly honest, the word *candidate* is from the Latin *candidus,* meaning "clean" or "pure." That's because in ancient Rome, political candidates wore white togas to impress the voters.

Common phrases may have unusual roots, too. When a person is grouchy all day, they are said to have gotten up on the wrong side of the bed. But why? Read on! The following is a celebration of the English language. It is a collection of word and phrase origins and meanings, as well as fun facts about the language that is spoken in more countries than any other.

FROM A TO Z

↪ The word *alphabet* comes from the first two letters used in the ancient Greek alphabet—*alpha* and *beta*.

↪ The use of the word *boss* became popular with American colonists, who didn't like the British custom of calling their employer "master." They preferred the Dutch word *baas,* which means "uncle."

↪ *Checkmate* is the term used when a player has won at chess by trapping the opponent's king. It is from the Persian phrase *shah mat,* which means "the king is dead."

↪ In the ancient Anglo Saxon language, *ang* means "painful" and *naegl* means "nail." Together, they have become the word *hangnail.*

*The magical term **hocus pocus** is taken from the name of a mythical Norse sorcerer, Ochus Bochus.*

↪ When pilots or sailors are in trouble, they may call out *"Mayday!"* over their radio. Although it's spelled differently, this distress call is from the French phrase *M'aidez,* which sounds just like *Mayday* and means "Help me!"

☞ At one time, Roman soldiers were paid for their work with a *salarium,* or ration of salt. As it became more difficult to provide the actual salt, the government paid the soldiers money with which to buy their own salt. Since then, a monetary payment in exchange for regular work has been called a *salary.*

☞ President Abraham Lincoln began his famous Gettysburg Address with the words "Four score and seven years ago." A *score* stands for the number 20. It is from a Nordic word meaning "cut" or "notch," because Nordic shepherds kept track of their herds by making a notch in a staff for every 20 sheep.

MIRROR IMAGE

A palindrome is a sentence or phrase that reads the same backward and forward. Study these, then try to make up some of your own.

A man, a plan, a canal—Panama.
Too hot to hoot.
No lemons, no melon.
Was it a car or a cat I saw?

WHAT'S IN A NAME?

The shortest sentence in the English language that uses every letter of the alphabet is, "Jackdaws love my big sphinx of quartz."

➤ Apparently, when one of the first Europeans visited Australia, he was fascinated by the large herds of leaping animals he saw. When he asked a local what they were called, the native responded *kangaroo*, which means "I don't know" in the Kanaka dialect.

➤ The state of *Nebraska* is named for an Oto Indian word that means "flat water." Although the Oto Indians could not have known it, millions of years earlier the entire state had, indeed, been underwater when a wide, shallow sea covered the central portion of the United States.

➤ The Canary Islands off the northwestern coast of Africa were named for dogs, not birds. The Romans named the island *insulae canariae*, or "island of dogs," for the packs of wild dogs that lived there.

FEARFUL WORDS

Clinophobia	Fear of going to bed
Cynophobia	Fear of dogs
Pogonophobia	Fear of beards
Scholionophobia	Fear of school
Scopophobia	Fear of being stared at
Sitophobia	Fear of food
Teratophobia	Fear of monsters
Triskaidekaphobia	Fear of Friday the 13th

WORD GAMES

 Can you name an eight-letter word that has only one vowel?
(See page 64 for answer.)

 Purple and orange are two words that don't rhyme with any other words. Can you think of others?

 Which letter of the alphabet is pronounced in the most different ways?
(Go to page 64 for answer.)

What Is That Thingamajig?

aglet: the metal tip on a shoelace
fillip: the sound made when you snap your fingers
kerf: the slit made by a knife or saw
lunula: the half-moon shape at the base of a fingernail
philtrum: the concave area between your nose and upper lip
rictus: the gap in the open beak of a bird

WHERE DID THAT COME FROM?

←

*"**G**ive someone the cold shoulder."* *During the Middle Ages, traveling knights would often stop for a rest and a meal at castles along the way. If the knight was welcome, he would receive a hot meal. If unwelcome, he would generally be given a cold shoulder of beef or mutton to eat. Now this phrase means to ignore someone.*

➤ **"Saved by the bell."** In 17th-century England, a guard at Windsor Castle was accused of falling asleep at his post and was sentenced to be executed. He claimed that he had been awake. To prove it, he said that the church bell had chimed an unusual 13 times at midnight on the night in question. Many townspeople testified that he was right. Since he must have been awake to hear

the strange occurrence, he was found innocent of the charge. The saying is now used to describe someone who has narrowly avoided serious consequences.

➤ **"An apple a day keeps the doctor away."** This saying originates from Roman times, when apples were believed to have magical powers that prevented one from becoming sick.

*"**B**ury the hatchet."* This phrase means to stop arguing and come to an agreement. It is from the Native American custom of burying weapons when a war was over.

➤ **"Let the cat out of the bag."** At one time, people at county fairs in the southern United States would sell small pigs and deliver them in sacks that were tied at the opening. Occasionally, a dishonest person would substitute a cat for the more valuable pig. Upon opening the bag, the customer would find out that he or she had been cheated. Today, this phrase means to reveal a secret.

➤ **"Get up on the wrong side of the bed."** In ancient Rome, it was thought to be unlucky to get out of bed on the left side. The Romans believed that if you did so, the rest of the day would not go well. Now, when people are grouchy all day, this phrase is used to describe their mood.

➤ **"Once in a blue moon."** A blue moon is the term used to describe the second full moon in one month. This only happens about every 32 months, so the saying refers to something that rarely happens.

"Shed crocodile tears." *When a crocodile opens its mouth, a reflex action causes tears to form in its eyes. These tears have nothing to do with pain or sorrow or any emotion at all. But this reflex is often noted when the crocodile is eating its prey. People who are said to shed crocodile tears are only pretending to be sad or sorry.*

"Turn someone down." During the 1800s, when a man proposed marriage, he would look into a "courting" mirror, then hand it to his girlfriend. If she looked at his reflection in the mirror, it meant she accepted. If she turned the mirror face down, she meant no, or was turning him down.

ANSWER PAGE

APPLES AND ORANGES, p. 10

First, take a piece of fruit from the box labeled Apples and Oranges. You know that this label is incorrect and there is only one kind of fruit in the box. If the piece of fruit you took out is an orange, then the box must be filled with oranges, so switch the label Apples and Oranges with the label on the box marked Oranges. Since you know that the other two boxes were also incorrectly labeled, the box that says Apples must also be wrong (remember, you haven't switched that one yet). Switch the Apples label with the label on the box now marked Apples and Oranges, and you'll have the correct labels on all three boxes!

SQUARE MATH, p. 9

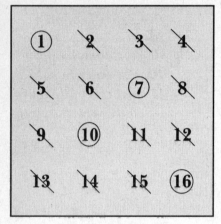

$$1 + 7 + 10 + 16 = 34$$

AND THE WINNER IS . . ., p. 10

The sons would have to switch horses. The winner is owner of the losing horse, so if they switched horses, each would try to cross the finish line first on his brother's horse.

DRIVE YOUR FRIENDS . . ., p. 10

The driver's eyes are the color of your friend's eyes, because your friend is driving the bus. You state that in the first sentence, but the person you are posing the question to usually gets so involved with trying to add and subtract passengers that he or she forgets what you said!

A PERFECT PAIR, p. 15

If you're lucky, two socks, but definitely not more than three. No matter what the combination, two of the three will match.

BOOK BITES, p. 16

You might think the answer is 6, but it's actually 2. When standing side by side, with the spines facing you, the first page of each volume is on the right side and the last page is on the left. To travel from the first page of volume one to the last page of volume three, the bookworm only needs to chew through volume two!

LOOK AT THE SENTENCE . . ., p. 16

Of course you can! I - T.

GOING UP?, p. 17

Ms. James is too short to reach the upper buttons.

SMALL CHANGE, p. 17

It sure would! But you might have to accept an IOU. The first day you'd earn 1¢, the second day 2¢, the third day 4¢, the fourth day 8¢, and so on. And remember that each of those days adds up (so, by the fourth day you would have 15¢). Believe it or not, by the end of the month, you would earn more than $10 million!

WORD GAMES, p. 61

First game: Strength
Third game: U as in busy, bury, thud, beautiful, burr, bull, and buy.